Mermaid
Wishes
and
Starfish Kisses!
xo
Maxine
Monterey Bay
California
2019

Follow Along at our Pebble Beach Site.
huckleberryhilladventure.com

Dear Mom and Dad,

My wish is that I can guide my Bella Sophia with the same amount of never ending encouragement, creativity, love and acceptance as you have given to me. This book, a complete work of love, is dedicated to my parents.

"I wished they would never stop squeezing me. I wished I could spend the rest of my life as a child, being slightly crushed by someone who loved me." – Ella Enchanted by Gail Carson Levine

To Nonna Frances Davi Cardinalli, Nonnu Salvatore Cardinalli and Great Auntie Mary Crivello. Grazie di cuore per tutto l'amore incondizionato che mi hai sempre donato. Spero che questo libro possa rispecchiare fedelmente la splendida e unica persona che sei. (Thank you for your gift of unconditional love. I hope this book captures your unique spirit.)

ISBN/SKU: 9780578464305
ISBN: 9780578464305

First Printing, 2019

Cover Design and illustrations by:

Drew McSherry
www.drewdrawart.com

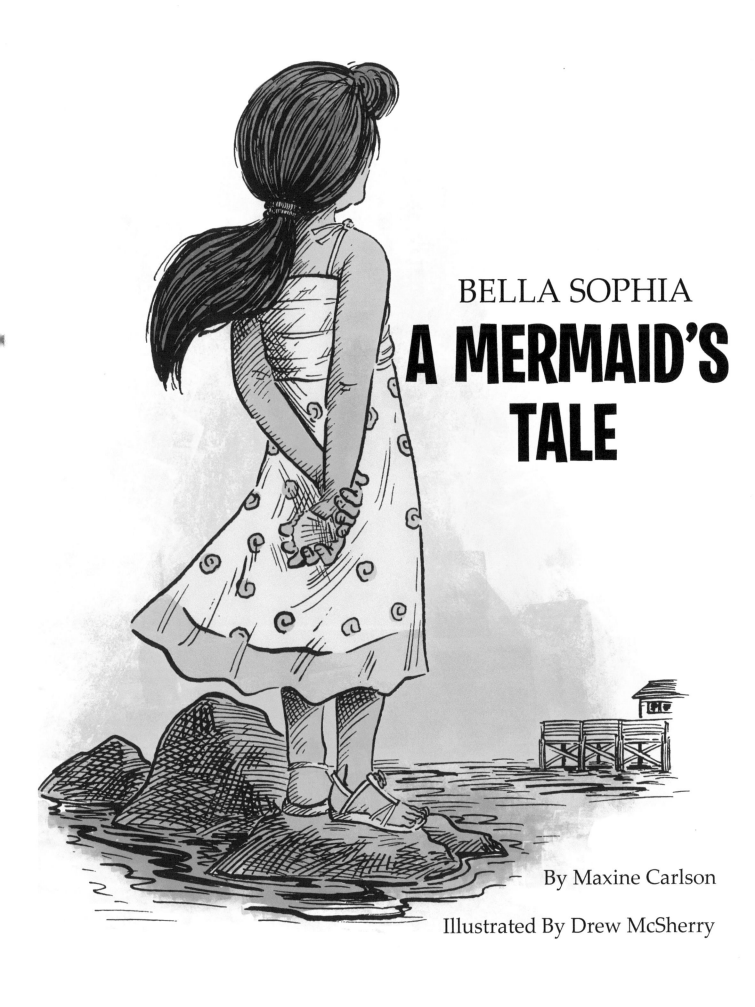

BELLA SOPHIA

A MERMAID'S
TALE

By Maxine Carlson

Illustrated By Drew McSherry

Part 1
-Helping Hands-

Ballerina style, Bella Sophia gracefully adjusts her pose, elongating her sturdy frame from tips of fingers to the very end of her extended toes. She calls out, "Nonna, did you say you wanted me to get a large platter?"

"Let me think," the older woman answers. "Uno, due, tre, quattro," Nonna is counting aloud, all the while organizing her stove top. The Sicilian dialect is accentuated by the clinking and clanking of pots and pans.

"Quattordici, fourteen of us for our regular supper. I love to see my entire family gathered around a traditional meal at least once a week. Let's set out two platters for couscous and two serving bowls for the stew," Nonna concludes.

"Dinner will be scrumptious," Bella Sophia answers. With grace beyond her years, she places colorful ceramic bowls delicately onto the counter.

Warm rays of afternoon light arched through the kitchen window highlighting a tin of exquisite saffron threads.

"My favorite perfumes are from nature," Bella Sophia deeply inhales the Mediterranean spices as she glances at the kitchen counter.

"Bella Sophia, the air will be even more fragrant. As soon as Auntie arrives we can transform semolina into couscous."

Frowning toward the bag of semolina, Nonna is realizing that hours of work lay ahead in preparation of the evening meal. "Grazie my bellissima, your helping hands and generous heart bless my kitchen. You are a good companion."

"I enjoy cooking with you too, Nonna," Bella Sophia replies. Besides, I am looking forward to being with family. It was a difficult week at school. I feel out of place there. I miss my cousins."

The oven timer makes Nonna suddenly jolt. The girl asks, "Nonna, are you startled?"

"Old habit," answers Nonna. "My ears are tuned to the cannery whistle. As you know, I worked in the factories on Cannery Row. The work of canning sardines was never ending. No time to even think just work, work, work. We all basked in the much needed income. Livelihood came into Monterey Bay with those tiny fish. It was a bustling time. Anyway, for cannery workers like me, that loud whistle was a signal to move quickly as our break had ended. I developed a practice of 'jumping to my feet' in response to loud noises."

"You are light on your feet! You still move fast," Bella Sophia encouraged with a grin.

The Hovden Cannery had closed down when Bella Sophia was all but a toddler. The noon time whistle had stopped with the final disappearance of sardines. For Bella Sophia, now a pre-teen, this was all a faint memory. The girl only had a fleeting recognition of this bygone era. However, it seems that the many years of factory work had forever imprinted into Nonna's daily habits.

"Old habits die hard," reasons Bella Sophia.

"Le vecchie abitudini sono dure a morire," Nonna repeats in Italian.

They heard a voice calling from afar. Looking toward one another they smiled, recognizing the familiar greeting of Auntie Mary's approach.

"Ciao. Ciao, Bella Sophia, help me… are you up there? It's slipping…assistance needed…down here!"

Bella Sophia glanced down from the high perch over Monterey Bay. Peeking between the huge fig tree and blackberry trellises, was one of her very favorite aunties! Bella Sophia could see a giant wooden sloped bowl balanced on the top of Aunty Mary's head.

"Go quickly and help her before she stumbles and falls," urges Nonna. "You would think she's married to that old couscous platter. We need her skilled hands."

Bella Sophia takes off, bolting down the long walkway. Transforming semolina flour into couscous is a laborious job. Bella Sophia smiles, grateful to have Auntie Mary's skilled hands join the efforts.

Nonna observes from the roof top deck, warning "careful … my basil."

At the foot of the steps Bella Sophia easily bounds over the basil seedlings. Skillfully shimmying she sways through the rows of herbs, racing around the old apricot tree, scurrying over lines of fava beans and darting past the Italian prunes. Breathlessly she runs to Auntie Mary at the ancient fig tree.

Minutes later, Auntie and Bella Sophia manage to lug the enormous couscous rolling bowl up the two flights of rickety stairs. The exhausted duo plopped down on deck chairs, "Mama-mia" they exclaim.

A bit winded, Auntie Mary inches closer to Bella Sophia, "How was school this week?" she asks.

Bella Sophia confides, "Auntie, I absolutely hated it! Awful, terrible. I am so glad it's the weekend! I never want to go back, I can't stand it there, it gets worse by the day. I want to stay home with my Nonna. The girls are so cruel. First it was the clothes I wore, teasing me that I wear hand sewn clothes. Then they laughed at the bows in my hair. Today, they said I have big, ugly, giant hands... and that no one will ever love me!"

Bella Sophia snuggles into Auntie's open embrace sinking down into the warm folds of her lap.

"Hold up your hands Bella Sophia," orders Auntie Mary.

Auntie Mary holds up her own hands to mirror Bella Sophia. "Frances, Frances come here," she cries.

Nonna rushes over.

"Frances hold up your hands," says Auntie Mary.

Now Bella Sophia, Auntie and Nonna are all comparing outstretched hands. "See," Auntie Mary continues. "You still have a way to go to catch up to us! Those girls are jealous. Pay them no attention."

Auntie Mary looked directly into Bella Sophia's eyes, "These hands, your hands," she squeezes Bella Sophia's hands for good measure, "these beautiful strong hands of yours are a blessing." Auntie Mary continues, "These hands will find and pick the ripest of figs."

"Hold a needle to make beautiful embroidery," adds Nonna.

"Cut pastina so fine to nourish babies," Auntie shares.

"Can tomatoes for a delicious sauce," contributes Nonna.

"Hold the books that will give you knowledge," nods Auntie.

"Count the rosary to say your prayers," asserts Nonna.

"And the best part," Nonna continues.

"The very, very, very best part," encourages Auntie Mary. "These wonderful, blessed beautiful hands will make the most delicious…"

"the most fabulous," sings Nonna.

"Couscous!" cheers Bella Sophia. "Let's get moving, we have lots of hungry mouths to feed."

The trio is busy pouring semolina grains slowly into a round terra-cotta dish. From an early age, Bella Sophia was taught that this special bowl with sloping sides, is called a 'mafaradda'. Mesmerized, the girl had observed her Nonna and Auntie transforming semolina into couscous for years.

When Bella Sophia turned seven, she learned the skill of forming the rough semolina into small pellets by hand. Her Auntie and Nonna were impressed, she took up the process and skills quickly. Bella Sophia had done well, over time she continued to watch and learn. The young girl copied the precise steps of the experienced women; hydrating, sifting, rolling, aerating, and forming the miniature pellets. This was all done by rolling her hands in choreographed fluid motions. Transforming the fine wheat semolina flour into beautiful mini couscous is called 'incocciata' by the Sicilians. For Bella Sophia this process felt like making magic with her hands.

Standing up to stretch her back Bella Sophia decides it's time to take a break. Her lungs filled with long satisfying deep breaths.

"I adore the scents of lavender, sweet basil, and salty ocean air," says Nonna, breathing in the hearty aroma from the garden below.

Auntie Mary agrees, "Pure delight to the senses. Accompanied by spiced saffron and the lamb stew bubbling away on your stove top. I am ravenous with hunger. This air is delightful."

"We've woken up the sea lions with the smell of dinner," laughs Nonna. Signaling sundown, the incessant barks of sea lions echoed across the bay. The animals always announce supper time with loud resonating grumbles.

"Bella Sophia," Nonna finally calls out. "We have enough couscous for tonight. Let's use these marvelous hands of yours to set the dinner table."

Part 2
-Mermaid Story-

"Delicioso," exclaims Uncle Vince.

"The best couscous ever!" chime cousins Paul and Joseph.

Bella Sophia glances around the room. The table is crowded with fourteen happy and satisfied faces. Some chatting, others drinking, an arm around a shoulder, a hand upon a hand, a spoon in a mouth and bread sopping up juices at the bottom of a plate. The couscous bowl long emptied, the stew devoured, the sweet spicy smell of saffron in the air. Fresh fruit, European marzipan, and whole nuts are being passed around the table. Grinning adults tilt tiny crystal glasses, filled with golden limoncello, toasting to good health. Under the setting sun, Uncle Frank takes out his pocket knife, grabs a shiny apple and removes the skin in one smooth circular motion. Baby Catherine squeals in delight and opens her tiny mouth ready for a sweet morsel. Little cousin Davey takes a glistening silver nutcracker and skillfully extracts walnut meat.

Twenty minutes later Nonnu Sal was seated in his favorite high-back chair. Bella Sophia is at his side. Little Francine is sitting eagerly up front wrapped in her blankie and sucking her thumb. Tiny Catherine and Davey lay underfoot awaiting this after supper story. Cousins Elizabeth and Maxine balance little Gianna on their laps, all eager for a tale.

Nonnu Sal begins, "This is true, it's our history. Our family is from the beautiful island of Sicily. Our town, Isola delle Femmine, the Island of Women, is on the south western side of the Mediterranean. Very close to Tunisia on the African continent. Sicily is an island of sunshine and citrus. All year long, the blossoms of blood oranges and lemons perfume the air. Our ancestors are descended from a long line of talented fishermen. For countless generations they would follow the catch between Sicily and Tunisia. The gentle waters of the Mediterranean made for an easy boat trip between the two fishing colonies. This allowed the men to provide a decent life for their families. Many years ago, before my great, great, great grandfather's time, the fishermen set off from their usual port off the pier of San Vito lo Capo, toward Tunis. While crossing the straight, the fishermen were faced with an unexpected storm. Tremendous gusts battered their vessel. Enormous waves knocked them to their knees. Torrents of battering rain and turbulent clouds cleared seagulls from the sky. The Mediterranean Sea had turned from calm water into a rage of tantrum waves. Before the men could get ashore, their boat capsized against a rocky break. The fishermen believed they were breathing their final breaths. They prepared to capsize. Each sailor felt alone, hopeless and lost.

Cutting through the howling wind came an unexpectedly sweet song of comfort and ease. In response to these heavenly voices the men suddenly calmed. Was this the prayer song of angels? Was the end near? An enormous wave overtook the boat. Falling overboard, the men submerged into froth and foam. Through rough seas melodic voices rose in volume calling each sailor toward saving arms. Every soul was gently guided ashore. All had all been saved. A true miracle, these magically appearing hands, had orchestrated a sudden rescue at sea. Amazed by this gift, each man gazed around the glorious bay of Tunis. Safe and secure on dry land, the fishermen dropped to their knees, thanking God and heaven for life and limb.

In the full moon light, as the fishermen glanced up from prayer, they noticed that they were surrounded by a beautiful sight. Smiling women looked upon them, it was obvious by their concerned expressions that they were worried for the downtrodden men. The women wanted to assist these battered gentlemen. The famished sailors were encouraged to follow the ladies ashore.

As the men rested along the sandy bank the aroma of delicious spices permeated the air. Observing the meal preparation, they noted that the bellissima women were not making traditional pasta. Under the moonlight, the rescued men watched in fascination as fine golden flour, looking like sparkling sand was poured into large trays. Skilled hands magically transformed this glistening fine mist. Synchronized in movement, the women worked, rolling, tossing, and sifting fine grain. The sight was transformative, an amazing vision as gifted hands made continuous movement, adding droplets of fragrant salt water in gentle sprinkles during the entire process. Looking closely, the fishermen notice that the hands of these talented women seem unique, almost a bit interconnected amongst the inner fingers. From a distance, it appeared similar to fine webbing or lace.

By this time the gentlemen were ravenous with hunger. The fright of the storm had weakened them. The women noted their still hungry expressions and called them over to eat.

The sailors had never experienced such delicious textures and exquisite flavors. They devoured the hand rolled wheat grains, now transformed to couscous flavored with saffron and thick nourishing stew, the most delicious meal ever. The fishermen instantly fell in love with both the aromatic food and the women. Overcome with these delights, they asked these strong skilled women to return to Sicily and marry them.

Romanced by the moonlight and the fine compliments of the handsome fishermen, the ladies too fell in love.

If these gentlewomen accepted the marriage proposal, they would have to reveal their most precious gift. So, after dinner the ladies invited the sailors to take a stroll toward the bay of Tunis. Under the full moon they gracefully dove into the warm salty sea.

As the women swam they sprouted long glittery fins. The fishermen were astonished! Aqua and teal shimmering tails splashed up for the Mediterranean making the warm waters froth with movement. The mermaids laughed and swam. Bounding up from the sea, their hands spread to reveal fine webbing between elegant fingers. The protected bay rolled and swayed with the aquatic acrobats of these gifted swimmers.

"God in heaven, angels on Earth, our lives have been saved by enchanted mermaids. They're glorious. Magnificent," cried the gentlemen in awe, now well enchanted by this rare sight.

These glorious mermaids accompanied their companions back to Sicily. Thrilled
with the rescue, the great Archbishop oversaw an elaborate wedding mass. The towns of Isola
de Femme and San Vito lo Capo came together, providing a grand reception with food, music
and a fancy tiered wedding cake. The next day, the mermaid women taught the Sicilian villagers
how to roll and make couscous. They shared Tunisian saffron and their delicious lamb stew
recipe. Their new families adored the foods and were impressed that the couscous was the
color of gold, just like a Sicilian sunset."

Nonnu looked at the children. All were completely engaged and enthralled by this story of their family history. The room echoed in stillness and silence, all absorbed in reflective thoughts.

Grinning from ear to ear, the grandfather was delighted that the little ones so enjoyed this legend. It is a true family tale and had been passed down for so many generations.

Standing quickly, Nonnu suddenly turned in circles and danced around his chair, making sure to look comically at his backside as he twisted and turned.

"Have ants in your pants?" Little Catherine teased Nonnu.

The kids started rolling on the floor laughing with hysterics.

"Nonnu!" shouted little Francine, "Why are you dancing in circles?"

"I'm chasing my rear end! Didn't you know that I was born with a tail!" he laughs.

The kids all dissolved into giggles, chanting "Nonnu is a merman! Nonnu is a merman!" The front room was alive with delightful vibrations of happiness and surprise.

While the other kids were distracted, Nonna takes Bella Sophia's hands into her and asks, "Bella Sophia… who are you?"

"I am a couscous eating mermaid!" she exclaims proudly opening her hands to look for webbing recognizing that her hands are not ugly at all. A warm light has been ignited within her heart, making her realize that her uniqueness, and each person's own gifts, is to be embraced.

Inspired, Bella Sophia extends her graceful hands up and out, reaching toward her cousins. Hand in hand, a family circle is quickly formed. A united rainbow of joined support. Minuscule hands grasp large hands. Dainty hands embrace rough hands. Wrinkled hands embrace smooth hands. All intertwined, all connected, all valued, all unique. Nonna and Bella Sophia are quickly encircled by a ring of delighted children. Grasping they raise their arms upward, skyward, past the stars and towards their dreams. With broad smiles they circle to the left, then sway to the right. In finale, the circumference of acceptance folds inwards embracing Nonna and Bella Sophia.

Bella Sophia's heart is on fire, warmed beyond measure with pride and joy.

About the Author

With deep Sicilian roots to Cannery Row in Monterey, California Maxine has carried down the tradition of cooking couscous. When her daughter, Bella Sophia, complains of feeling "under the weather," Maxine can be overheard informing her daughter that she must be missing salt water, her tail needs to come out for a bit of fun.

The Wild Buck (Book One of the Huckleberry Hill Adventure Series) is the author's first book. This book was recognized with a Gold Medal Moonbeam Award (2017) for exemplary children's literature and merchandise. For recipes, author events and new book release information follow along at the author's popular Pacific Coast blog: huckleberryhilladventure.com.

About the Illustrator

Drew's artistic journey began around the age of five with a favorite activity of copying illustrations from the Ed Emberley series of drawing books. As his skills and passion developed Drew pursued a Bachelor of Arts Degree in Graphic Design from Loyola Marymount in Los Angeles. He then pursued a more traditional art avenue via The Academy of Art University in San Francisco earning a Masters of Art Degree in Fine Art with a focus on Children's Book Illustration. A few years after graduation, Drew met his encouraging wife (who happened to be a journalist for National Public Radio). They soon combined their talents to write a series of children's books based around shapes, teaching students the fundamentals of drawing and geometry. From there Drew began illustrating his own books and partnering with authors on their projects.

About San Vito lo Capo, Sicily, Italy

A couscous festival takes place every year, towards the end of September, in the lovely Mediterranean town of San Vito lo Capo, Sicily. A worldwide famous celebration, honoring and recognizing the different cultures that have influenced the Sicilian people and affected the southern Italian way of life. World-famous chefs gather in this tiny town with its gorgeous white sandy beach to engage in a couscous culinary contest. Each chef presents their best re-interpretation of this ancient Arabic recipe. Locals and tourists alike sample countless versions of this dish. In many ways, couscous symbolizes the historical influences of the island's culture, people and traditions.

-BELLA SOPHIA'S BOOK CLUB-

Bella Sophia and the mermaids invite you to reflect on the following questions. Perhaps on your own (or while in the bath as you soak your tail). Best yet, when chatting with friends during a delightful couscous supper party.

1. The story is set in Monterey Bay, California during the late 1970's. The book is based on the author's real life experience. What do you think the coastal town looked like during this time? Include key locations such as Cannery Row, the Pacific Ocean and Nonna's garden.

2. Plant a virtual dream garden. What favorite fruit trees, vegetables, herbs or flowers would you include? Will you add a bee hive for honey or support wild life with bird feeders? Will your garden have a tranquil water feature or relaxing sitting area? How about adding in a tree house for a garden 'get-a-way.' Dream big!

3. Bella Sophia shares with her Aunt that she feels teased and 'out of place' at school. What advice would you give Bella Sophia that might help her heal her broken heart? If you attended her school what steps could you take to help her?

4. How is couscous connected within both sections of this two-part story? In 'Helping Hands' do you think it was difficult for Bella Sophia to hand make couscous? In 'Mermaid Story' did you notice that the mermaids were able to transform sand grains into semolina flour? How does couscous connect part one and two of the book?

5. What are your favorite colors and illustrations from the book? How would you draw mermaids? How would you style their tails? How do you think mermaids wear their hair? What objects from the sea could mermaids use to make jewelry?

6. Design the mermaid's and fisherman's wedding cake. How many tiers? What flavors? Think of creative decorations that might connect the cake to the ocean.

7. Compare Bella Sophia's inner self confidence from the beginning of the story to the end. She takes you on an emotional journey. How has her confidence grown? How does she see herself at the end of the book?

-Mermaid Bath Soak-

Add 2 cups Epsom salt and ¼ cup olive oil to your bath. Epsom salt added to a warm bath tub helps you to relax and ease muscles. Adding olive oil to your Epsom salt bath will condition and soften skin (a mermaid must keep her tail well hydrated). Relax and enjoy!

-Couscous Recipe-

My Godmother, Christina Davi D'Aquanno keeps Sicilian tradition alive with this Tunisia inspired recipe. Her brother Tom, takes after the family legacy as an exceptional fisherman, spending many summers in the waters off Alaska. Siblings Christina and Tom are both creative Sicilian cooks.

My Godmother Christina, holds this recipe very close to her heart. This dish is "as remembered" passed down to her via her father Gaetano "Tom" Davi, who learned it from his mother (Francesca Lucido Davi). Christina shared this recipe with me, and I am thrilled to publish our family version of 'couscous de Tunisia'. Parina (Godmother) Christina and I both have a passion for archiving Sicilian culture and traditions.

While traveling frequently through Sicily, Christina and her husband Frank D'Aquanno have sampled many couscous variations; many with sea food. In Sicily, it is very common to serve the Trapanese style couscous with freshly prepared fish. Each region has a certain style for presenting couscous at the family table. The couscous and lamb stew combination is delicious and a signature dish of my Davi clan, influenced by their time spent in Tunisia. Chicken can easily be substituted for the lamb in this hearty stew. A delicious vegetarian version of the recipe is also provided, as veggie stew is my daughter, Bella Sophia's favorite accompaniment to couscous.

Further recipes can be found at huckleberryhilladventure.com.

-Couscous da Tunisia-
-Tunisia Inspired Couscous-

Serves 4 people

Ingredients:

6 cups water
1 head of cabbage, quartered
3-4 carrots, peeled and cut into two inch pieces
2 bell peppers (any variety; green, yellow, red or mixed) cut into strips
1 turnip, peeled and cut into fourths (quartered)
4-6 pounds of lamb necks (**or 4-6 pounds of chicken thighs, not skinless)
2 large strands or 3 medium strands of good quality saffron
1 (15 oz.) can of garbanzo beans
Sea salt and ground pepper to taste
** The original recipe calls for lamb. The use of chicken thighs is an alternative version.

Couscous:

Hand making couscous is a learned skill. For this recipe use one 10 oz. (283g) box of original couscous mix. It cooks in five minutes. Make according the package directions, fluff with a fork and set aside. The couscous will be served with the stew.

Steps:

Cut off extra fat from the protein

In a heavy duty stew pot, over medium heat, sauté protein in olive oil until both sides are evenly browned

Add water

Add saffron threads to water and protein. Cover and lower temperature to simmer for 2 hours (or until tender)

Add turnips and carrots

Continue to let simmer for additional 30 minutes (or until tender)

Add cabbage and bell peppers and simmer for an additional 30 minutes (or until tender)
Before serving and while the stew is on the stovetop add in garbanzo beans.

To Serve Couscous with Stew:

Fluff couscous with a fork. For each person add a layer of couscous to the bottom of a large plate. Top with stew. Enjoy this traditional Sicilian dish.

-Veggie Stew-

Bella Sophia's favorite variation.

Step One: For this recipe use one 10 oz. (283g) box of couscous mix. It cooks in five minutes. Make according to the package directions, fluff with a fork and set aside. The couscous will be served with the stew. Add one drained can (8 oz.) of organic garbanzo beans, gently combine garbanzo beans to the cooked couscous. Set aside.

Serves 4-6 people

Ingredients:

4 large zucchinis, peeled and cut into round slices
1 large sweet onion, peeled and cut into small pieces
2 large Mediterranean eggplants, not peeled and cut into small cubes
2 (8 oz.) cans diced organic tomatoes (San Marzano)
1 (4 oz.) tube organic tomato paste
6 cups organic vegetable broth
2 strands high quality saffron threads, seeped in ½ cup of warm water
4 tbsp. chopped fresh basil
1/2 tbsp. ground black pepper

1 dash ground nutmeg
1 pinch sea salt
1 ½ cups fresh organic mild chunky salsa
2 cups frozen organic peas
6 TBS. olive oil (this is to sauté the onion, eggplant and zucchini)

Steps:

In a large heavy duty stew pot add 4 TBS. olive oil, start to brown onion to caramelize (about 3 minutes cooking time over medium heat) as this first step adds dimension to the dish.

Add 2 additional TBS. olive oil to the onion, continue cooking over medium heat while adding in the zucchini and eggplant to combine (about 4 additional minutes cooking time).

Add the remaining ingredients (except frozen peas), and bring to a boil.

Reduce heat to low and let simmer, stirring frequently in a covered pot until vegetables are tender and to let flavors expand (1 hour).

The final 10 minutes, before serving, add 2 cups of frozen organic peas.

Open and drain the garbanzo beans. Fluff cooked couscous with a fork and toss in beans.

For each serving add a layer of couscous to the bottom of a large plate. Top with vegetable stew.

Enjoy this traditional Sicilian dish.

CPSIA information can be obtained
at www.ICGtesting.com
Printed in the USA
BVHW050930290519
548856BV00002B/3/P